DANIELLE BROOKS

Sweet Like Sundays
A Romance Novella

Copyright © 2024 by Danielle Brooks

All rights reserved. No part of this publication may be reproduced, stored or transmitted in any form or by any means, electronic, mechanical, photocopying, recording, scanning, or otherwise without written permission from the publisher. It is illegal to copy this book, post it to a website, or distribute it by any other means without permission.

This novel is entirely a work of fiction. The names, characters and incidents portrayed in it are the work of the author's imagination. Any resemblance to actual persons, living or dead, events or localities is entirely coincidental.

First edition

ISBN: 9798876623041

This book was professionally typeset on Reedsy. Find out more at reedsy.com

This book is dedicated to all the lovers who need the reminder that romance is still tangible.

Author Note

So we are here. This moment that I am writing my Author Note for my very first publication is surreal. I've fantasized about this since I was a young girl in Rockville, VA, writing in five-subject notebooks, and here I am, greeting you, lovers. Thank you for choosing my book to dive into a world of romance. I hope this book gives you all the feels, a little spice, but most importantly, the idea that romance is still real, available, and attainable. I look forward to continuing to have you on the romance journey with me.

Keep in touch.
You can find me on all social platforms as @DanielleBrooksWrites

I

First Sunday

Sade

I wake up my phone, swipe to find my music, and click on the "Sunday Vibes" playlist, signaling it to play on shuffle. Anita Baker's "Caught up In A Rapture" begins to play through the soundbar mounted on the wall under my flat screen TV, on-brand for the vibe I'm in today, relaxed, renewed, and ready to do some spring cleaning. It never fails; at the turn of the season, I am always intuitively led to do a good deep clean of my home, getting the baseboards, wiping down the ceiling fans, checking my closets for things I no longer need, and this first Sunday of April feels like the perfect day to do so. The sun is already beaming over a bright blue sky, making being up at 8 am on a Sunday not so bad.

In the background, I can hear my coffee maker humming into its start in brewing my choice of coffee this morning, a rich nutty hazelnut, and as the aroma begins to meet my nose, I tighten my floral satin robe around my waist. I make my way to my front door, opening it and the storm door to reach out and into my old squeaky mailbox for the mail for the week. I make a mental note to go to my local hardware store and find a new mailbox while my heart sinks at the thought of replacing this one. The home I live in here in Stonecrest is my grandparents' home, which I affectionately referred to as my grandmother's home, as she ran this home and everyone in it with her eyes closed. Everything about the exterior, including its bright turquoise color, white paneling, and this old, rickety mailbox, is like she left it when she passed four years ago. I planned to keep the home's exterior intact, especially the color, as I love how it brightens my mood when I come home and, most importantly, for the nostalgia of my grandparents. However, I don't think this old mailbox is a significant change; it's just a little modernization and a piece of me.

I flip through the mail, sorting out the essential pieces and trashing the fluff, placing the pieces I want to keep on my little round wooden table that sits in the middle of the kitchen, moving on to prep my coffee with a splash of caramel and a healthy splash of vanilla almond creamer. I stir the creamer with a teaspoon until my coffee is light brown and take a sip of the hot coffee, satisfied with the taste. I place the mug onto the kitchen table and begin my Sunday morning routine. Walking back through the kitchen and into the adjoining living room, I open the bay windows that my couch sits against and then place one of my slides between the front door and the storm door to leave a small crack and then proceed to the fireplace mantle on the east wall of the living room. I grab my bundle of sage, light it, and allow the poignant scent of the thick smoke to permeate the room. I hit a quick two-step as Maze's "Can't Get Over You" starts to play before making my way through the rest of my home, spreading the clearing smoke of the sage through every room, hitting each corner, and opening windows as I do so. Many hate the smell of sage, but as for me, I love it. It gives me the sense of starting fresh and new, wiping away anything that's not serving me for the upcoming week, a great beginning to my morning of cleaning.

My Spring cleaning will only take me the morning. This is my first Spring here in Stonecrest, as an adult, that is. I used to come here often as a kid to spend weekends with my grandparents, and back then, Stonecrest was a small rural town with a few homes, a post office, a library, and a local grocery store. Now, it's a bustling suburban neighborhood town thanks to developers coming in and buying up land. We even have a few local businesses and an entire grocery store amongst the new subdivisions sprinkled throughout the town. After my grandmother passed, I inherited the home, but I didn't move in until last January, right after the New Year, and when I came back to

Stonecrest, it was bittersweet seeing how much it had changed. I'm thankful, however, that several other families that were part of the original Stonecrest area and I have stood firm on keeping their homes and land. Everyone in the few blocks surrounding me is an original homeowner or at least a family member of the originals.

By noon, I have finished cleaning my home, steam mopping all of the wooden floors in the kitchen, my room, and the spare room I use as my zen room. The full bathroom in my room and the hallway consist of white pebble tile floors that I mop with natural ingredients to preserve authenticity. As I survey the rooms, all bright in color and now scented with the fragrance of orange, lavender, and lemon thanks to the new fragrance warmers I installed in each room, I take in all the things that remind me of my grandparents, along with the blend of modern furniture and appliances that add a piece of me. I smile with satisfaction with what I've accomplished today and over the past year.

With the most taxing part of my day done, I was ready for my favorite part of Sunday: time in my garden. After a refreshing shower, throwing on a white tee-shirt and a pair of old denim shorts, I transfer my Sunday tunes to my portable speaker and place it on the metal garden table that was painted white just outside the back door leading to the backyard. My soothing soul music has now moved into smooth Neo-Soul as Jill Scott croons, "He Loves Me." I smile at how in tune my soul and the music are today and proceed to the little garden that has been here since my grandparents were alive to check on the seasonal fruits and a few plants I now have sprouting up.

Gardening is something I picked up from spending time with my grandmother. She did it as another way to source her food, and while it still serves that purpose for me, it's become a therapeutic pastime. Getting into my garden on Sundays allows me to put my hand in some soil and get grounded, remember my being and my soul when busy weeks can make you forget that you are a human and not a robot. I'm blessed that work life isn't super stressful for me, as on top of this home, when my grandmother passed, I found that I also inherited a trust that she held onto that was from my grandfather. In her will, she said that Grandpa Winston left her in possession of the trust, and when she passed, it would be released to me; even my mother was shocked by this information. It was enough for me to pursue opening my wellness spa two years ago. It's small, but the perfect size for me, and it booms with business from people who value holistic wellness through yoga, meditation, energy healing, and the like. To know I'm serving for the greater good of humanity feels good.

I was so engrossed in picking the few bushels of strawberries and lemons that I didn't even notice that my neighbor had come outside. It wasn't until I heard the clang of metal hit the pavement. The sound startles me, and I turn in the direction of the sound, my eyes making direct contact with him. He stands in front of the barbell and large weights he just dropped, his sepia skin glistening with beads of sweat dripping down the curves of his pectoral muscles. His basketball shorts are set right at his hip, revealing the cut of muscle at the bottom of his abdomen leading to his groin. I would be behooved to say this man was not fine. His face is clear of blemishes, like he keeps himself hydrated, and his dark, thick facial hair and flowing mane that grew from his head, which he usually keeps in a ponytail that's wrapped down with a black string, showed that he was not unmindful of hair care either. I release an unexpected breath at the sight of this specimen of a man. He shoots me a crooked smile, and I nervously send him a smile back, hoping he does not grasp my obvious observation of his physique.

"Miss Sade," he greets me with a nod, his deep baritone slow with a thick Southern drawl. His accent is intoxicating, along with his Colgate smile. His smile, surrounded by deep pink lips, complements his rich brown skin. I almost forgot that he was greeting me with my middle name, which he believed was my first name. I dust off my dirt-clad hands on my shorts, hoping it would also shake off the hypnotism.

"Hey, Ace." I wave at him and place my hands on my hips. "You make me feel like a little old lady with that 'miss,' *Mister*." I purse my lips at him but then let out a soft chuckle. He winces at my salutation but then joins my laughter as if he understands the sentiments of feeling old with the formality being put back on him. He pushes back the sweat that tempts to fall from his forehead. The air was still crisp, but Ace was sweating profusely.

"I guess we're both over here feeling like some old Mister and Misses, huh?"

I nod my head in agreement, and my smile brightens. "You look like you need a little cooling off. I have some fresh lemonade if you like."

"I could use a break and a drink." He grabs a small hand towel that he had tossed on the ground and wipes his forehead, chest, and arms down before making his way over.

Ace

As if she can't get any more beautiful, seeing her this afternoon proves her beauty has no defying level. I don't see her often outside of our chance meetings on Sundays like today, and even with remnants of soil on her cheek, she's beautiful. Perhaps what makes her even more stunning is that she doesn't mind getting her hands dirty with a task that also brings out the patience one must have when gardening. I watch her quickly saunter off into her home. I meet her in her yard just as she comes out with two glasses filled with ice and lemonade. It takes me three gulps to finish the glass of the perfect balance of sweet and sour, and it sends an immediate cooling through my body.

"I can fill you up again," She offers, extending her hand to take my glass.

I wave off the offer. "No, ma'am. Have a seat and enjoy your lemonade. I'll munch on this ice. It's really what I need." I allow her to sit first before I join her at the patio table. I look over her garden, observing how much it has grown over the year she's been here. I've silently watched her from afar, tending to her garden. The way her harvest flourishes, I could tell she had a nice green thumb and a nurturing soul. "I see your garden growing nicely."

A bashful smile grows on her face, causing her round cheeks to rise, giving her face an angelic glow. Her gaze wanders over her work. "Yeah, it is. I have some strawberries and lemons now, and my plant babies are growing, too." She fawns over her accomplishments like they are her natural children, and I think it's cute."

The sounds of Jill Scott's "Golden" fill the airwaves, and I nod my head to the beat of the song, tossing back a few pieces of ice into my mouth. I crunch on them and allow the ice chips to trickle down my throat for another wave of coolness through my body. "My girl, Jill. You keep a nice vibe over here. I'm sometimes surprised at some of the old school you play."

She leans back in her chair and screws her face in confusion. "How so?" Sipping from her glass, I notice a drop of juice journey down her full bottom lip. She licks her lip, swiping the runaway liquid, leaving her lip glistening from her saliva with the help of the sun beaming down. My eyes narrow at the beauty of her glistening lips.

I adjusted my vision back to her eyes, remembering that she did ask me a question in response to my attempt to tease her. "You don't look old enough to know anything about soul artists like Anita, let alone Chaka." I am teasing her. She doesn't look that much younger than me, but since we are conversing more than we've had over the last year of being neighbors, I use it to inquire about how close we are.

"Psshh," she blows through her lips. "First, I'm an old lady, and now I'm a teeny bopper?!" She gives me a serious look, and I gawk, realizing my offense. She spills into a laugh, letting me know she didn't take my words to heart. "I'm playing. But I doubt I'm that much younger than you."

"Oh yeah? Amuse me."

"A lady never tells her age," she sasses, raising her right eyebrow twice, challenging me.

I chuckle at her cuteness. "You're right. Well, I'm 35," I rub my hand through my beard in thought. "So, I'd say you're at least that, give or take a year or two."

"I'm 34." Her face screams that she is impressed. 'Looks like you are, in fact, that old man here."

We laugh in unison at her clapback, and I am happy to know she has a sense of humor. It's attractive to see a woman laugh freely and not take offense to a small, innocent joke. It doesn't hurt that her smile is infectious at its biggest and brightest point. I nod at her clapback, admitting her checkmate. "You got me. I'll take that one."

Our laughter collides and then drifts into silence, leaving only the birds chirping and the leaves light rustling. The music continues to shuffle between new and old R&B classics. We pick up a chill conversation about minuscule topics, from the weather to the building of a new business in Stonecrest.

"Man, I remember when none of this was here. I kinda miss "small town" Stonecrest," Sade reminisces. She gets comfortable in her seat just as much as her memories, propping her bare feet onto the empty patio chair. I notice they are perfectly pedicured and painted in soft bubblegum pink, and although she's been outside in her garden, they show a soft sheen from a layer of lotion. I bit the inside of my lip, taking in her pretty feet, and then towards her, giving my attention to her words.

"I heard it was a little different than it is now."

"*A lot* different. I inherited my house from my grandparents. They built this from the ground up when Stonecrest was nothing but land and that grocer at the corner of Manger Road. That's how I remember Stonecrest from when I was a little girl coming to visit."

Her admission fills in the blanks of her moving into the cottage home. When I saw her moving in, I was confused about why she chose Stonecrest. I remember the day like it was yesterday because I was perplexed at how I ended up with a fine sista in a home next to mine in this slow suburban neighborhood. She was moving some gardening items into the small shed under a big willow tree in the middle of our properties. I remember everything about her from that day. She wore a blue and red head wrap that pulled her curly fro to the top of her head, a white shirt, and a flowing blue skirt. Very bohemian. Then again, maybe she would move to a town like this, but she looked nothing like the rest of the community of elders and middle-aged families. I guess she could've thought the same thing about me, too.

"That makes sense as to why you're here." My words trail out of my mouth without much thought.

"*Despite it all*, it's a nice place to be." She lets out a dry laugh, catching my underlying joke. She places her eyes on me, briefly looking me up and down.

"What brings you here? You look like a city slicker."

I bellow out a laugh at the nickname. "Funny, my pops calls me that...city slicker. My Pops owned the house." I nod in the direction of my pale yellow rancher. "I have the deed now since he decided to take it easy in Florida a few years back. You know how old folks like moving South when they retire."

"Mmhmm," she hums, sipping what was now water from the melting ice in her cup.

"I guess you can say I'm a "city slicker." I lived in downtown Regency before coming out here, but when the developers came sniffing around here, I came to keep an eye on things and let them know we can't be bought.

"I know that's right," Sade chimes in. "I'm glad that so many of the original owners or at least family members of them are still here. Yeah, it's slower than Regency, but our community is filled with so much history and land owned by *us*, and you know there's not much of that around nowadays."

I nod my head, growing more intrigued about Sade through her insight. She's right; owning land as an African American was a big thing to our elders and is being understood by our generation even more now. Hearing her talk about the importance of owning land and property was hella attractive to me, seeing that the beauty of her mind matches her outer beauty.

I feel the buzz of my phone's silent ringer against my thigh and reach to retrieve it. As if he could, since I am talking about him, my weekly call from my Pops is coming through. I sit, pondering if I should take the call at this very moment as I am enjoying this unanticipated time with Sade. I only talk with Pops once per week, so I decided to take the call.

"I hate to cut this short, but my weekly check-in with my Pops awaits." I wave the still-vibrating phone with my Pops picture as proof.

"Oh, by all means, take it. My Sunday self-care awaits anyway." She flashes me an understanding smile, collects the cups, and heads into her home. I catch a glimpse of her petite yet bubble backside as she walks off, paying attention to the cuffs of her cheeks peeking from the bottom. I try to remain a gentleman by releasing my dirty thoughts with a rough breath. I accept the call from my Pops.

"Hey, what's up, Pops."

"Hey Aeran, I thought I was going to miss ya for a second. You *know* my time is limited." He chuckles at the end of his statement.

My Pops swears he is still that guy, but if I'm honest, he probably is handling business out there in Florida. My Pops was what they call a rolling stone in his earlier years, hence why we didn't have a real relationship until I was about 17 years old, but if I can be truthful again, that had to be the best time of my life to begin my relationship with him. Was he always right in how he moved when I was younger? No. But having him at the height of me going from boy to man and at the time in his life when he was learning from his mistakes made it easier for me to understand and learn from him. Because of that time and our growth over the years, he is easily one of my best friends.

"Yea, yea, I know, pops. You got a whole wild life out there in Florida," I say sarcastically. I open my back door and walk into my kitchen. I am welcomed by the cool air blast that central air provides. I grab a water bottle from my fridge and settle at the kitchen table. "I was outside talking to my neighbor."

"Oooh, you finally stopped being a punk and talked to that girl, eh?" He snickers at his correct assumption, but I wasn't about to tell him immediately that he was right.

"Now, Pops, you know there's nothing punk about my 235-pound ass." I flex my perfectly pumped pectorals one at a time as if he could see my actions. "But why does it have to be her? Maybe I was having a conversation with Ms. Jeannette."

"Everybody knows you don't have to have a conversation with Jeannette because she knows everything before we do." I burst out laughing at the facts Pops just spoke. "But I know it was that girl. You ain't take that long to answer for no, Ms. Jeannette, unless you like them wrinkled and on their way out." He's now cackling at his joke, and I can't help but continue to laugh with him.

"Anyway, Pops," I say, settling out of my laughing fit. "I was out there talking with her, Sade."

"Sade, huh? Does she look like Sade, too?" I knew instinctively he was referring to the infamous singer, Sade.

"Mmm, she'd give Sade a run for her money," I confess, my thoughts returning to the image of her beautiful sun-kissed face from this afternoon.

She could give any woman a run for their money in my eyes, and that's facts. I'm no man who judges a woman and what she decides to do to make her feel good, but so many women nowadays are getting fillers here and fillers there. And I'm not opposed to makeup, but from my understanding, makeup is supposed to enhance your face and not make a whole new face. But Sade, I've always seen her with what I think is her in all her naturalness, but not in an I-don't-take-care-of-myself kind of way. Her eyebrows are always shaped well, her skin glowing, her lips tantalizing and moist. Simply put, she exudes her natural beauty and would be hard to fake or cover up.

"About time. Now I can get a daughter-in-law so you can come down and not be a third wheel to all my dates." My jokester of a dad rolls out another round of laughter at himself, and I shake my head and muffle my laughter.

"You a wild boy, Pops. You're going to have to wait a while for that. I barely know her to be talking about making her a wife."

"It's never too early to be thinking about it, though. Life and love are fleeting. Don't miss out on either of them or before you know it, you will be my age, still dating like you are young. That's one thing I regret, not settling down and enjoying the kind of life I'm trying to enjoy now with someone I love." His side of the line grows silent, and my heart drops a little at my dad's words.

My Pops is 75, going on 76 this June, and never married any of the women he had in his life, including my mother, but when he talks, I know he wishes he had married my mother before she got tired of waiting for him to grow up. He was 40 years old when I was born and still fighting his youth and growing up. Sometimes, I think that after my mom moved on and even more after she passed, he gave up on settling down and just continued to be the bachelor he was then and still is. He's a youthful 75, still takes care of himself, socializes, and still gets women, but I don't think he will ever settle, especially at this age and how he speaks about it.

"It's never too late for you either, Pops," I say with seriousness, cloaked in a slight chuckle.

"Shiit," he says, his voice pepping up. "At this point, I'm gonna die with one or two women by my side." I hear him slap his leg as he laughs again, straight from his chest. I join him again and shake my head at my dad's humor.

However, his prior words still echo in my head. *Life and love are fleeting. Don't miss out on either one of them....*

II

Second Sunday

Ace

When I awoke to the sun beaming through my window, I gave a fist pump to the air and sent up a word of gratitude. The one thing I despise about Spring is that all the rain magically decides to pour during April. This past week felt like a monsoon decided to come through and double back for reassurance of its presence with rain nearly the whole week. It made for an up-and-down week of business at auto detailing shops that I took over for my Pops, but a hell of a weekend for cutting the grass this weekend.

Not wanting to prolong the task of manicuring my yard, I decided now was the time to start moving. The earlier, the better in my book to ensure I get my outdoor workout in. I could go to a gym, but it's nothing like inhaling the fresh spring air while pumping some iron. The air feels new and clean going into my body as opposed to the stuffy, humid air in the weight room of the gyms, in my opinion. After getting all this rain this weekend, I'm sure the pollen has been swept away, too, yet another up for the week of downpours.

I roll over and sit up, settling my feet on the cool wooden floor. I give myself a moment to fully wake up, stretching my back and arms to their max. The home is quiet besides the low hum of the refrigerator running.

"That's one thing I regret, not settling down and enjoying the type of life

I'm trying to enjoy now with someone I love.."

The thought of the conversation Pops and I had last week comes to mind, and in that moment, I realize that Pops legit lived in this home alone, with the same deafening quietness. Now, I'm sure Pops had his share of women. Still, in the grand scheme of things, Pops did most of his life as a single man without a complete family in a home equipped to house a family of at least four, considering the main bedroom and another bedroom that I could imagine could suit two children. Instead, when I moved in, the two rooms were set up as a bachelor's suite and a junk room, with no sight of a woman's touch anywhere. Is there anything much different now that I'm here? Not really. The junk room is now just a sparsely furnished room with a TV and loveseat I used to lounge in. And my room…it's equipped with the bare minimum, a king-sized bed with black linen, a dresser, light, literally, the bare minimum. *Am I turning into Pops?* The thought rushes me, and I can feel a slight panic hit my core.

It can't be denied that Pops lived a life you'd want to live vicariously through. Still, after it all is said and done, even he said he wished he had developed that family unit, at least settled down with a forever love, and as single as I am now, I want to settle down with my forever and always love…one day. The faint sounds of future children running the halls and the scent of buttered pancakes and crispy bacon invade my imagination, painting the picture of what a forever love and family look like for me. It quickly diminishes as I hear the creaking of a door open from outside of my opened window. Through my vertical blinds, I could see Sade stepping onto her front porch, her body clad in a satin pink and floral robe that fell just below her backside. Her curves peek through the robe but still keep enough for the imagination. She stands there momentarily, her curly fro billowing like a fluffy cloud exposing the radiant sun, her beautiful bare face being the sun. I shutter at her beauty. She tilts her head back and closes her eyes, seeming to absorb the same freshness I'm waiting to experience. When she turns in my direction, I jump as if she could see me peering at her. To my relief, she reached into the mailbox on the side of her home, grabbed her mail, and returned inside. I laugh at myself and worry about her catching me watching her. In reality, the way the blinds were half open, she couldn't see my truth. I return my thoughts to the task of the morning and get dressed in a white undershirt, basketball shorts, and sneakers.

Stepping into my backyard, I decided to start cutting there first out of convenience as the push mower is stored in the shed in the backyard. As I run the mower down my last row of unkempt grass, I look over to Sade's yard, which had grown naturally from the week of rain, too. A generous idea sparks my mind, and I turn off the mower and head to her back porch.

Sade

I hear the sound of knocking at my door, masked under the tunes of Sampha playing through my speakers. I wrap my robe around my damp body and head to the back door with an expression of puzzle and wonder on my face. That look turns into surprise as my eyes widen, and my heart skips a beat at the sight of Ace. It wasn't because I was afraid, but because ever since our encounter last week, he has created this effect on me out of nowhere. Last week was the most conversation we had with each other and the closest we've ever been regarding vicinity. Although the conversation was short, it was a depth that allowed me to learn more about him and some of our similarities. It didn't help that being in such proximity to him gave me a better view of how gorgeous of a man he was, from his smooth skin to his sharp jawline and facial features. This morning, through the glass of my back door, he looks just as appealing, even in his damp undershirt and hair pulled into a puff at the back of his head.

"Ace, hey," I greet through a breath, ensuring that the belt of my robe is secure enough and I am covered.

"Good Morning." I see him glance over me quickly before returning his eyes to mine. I grow flush at his observation of me. "I was mowing the lawn and noticed your lawn. I don't mind getting your lawn while I'm doing mine.. if that's okay with you?"

I peer past him and notice the long grass covering my backyard, and then back at Ace, who stands in front of me with doe eyes filled with sincerity, waiting for my reply. I'm actually kind of shocked at his generosity, not that this seems out of the ordinary; I could tell that he was a gentleman by his mannerisms and that god-awful reference to me as "Miss" last week. Having a man offer to do this is…different for me. I usually mow my lawn, but with it being a rainy week, business was unusually busy with people taking advantage of some indoor relaxation at the spa, making me one exhausted person this weekend. I even started my Sunday self-care much later than usual. I hadn't even thought about my lawn. Taking him up on his offer sounds nice.

"Wow, Ace, sure, that would be nice. I hadn't even thought about my yard yet today."

"Not a problem, Miss Sade. A woman shouldn't have to do this type of yard work anyway. I gotcha covered."

Ace moves on before he can see the stars sparkling in my eyes, hear my soft exhale, and experience the hearts flying around my body. Although imaginary, I felt they were real enough to see through the expression of admiration and surprise that took over my face. *Chivalrous.* I learned that about him today, and it tugs at my soul..in a good way. Far too often, men meet the physical requirements but lack chivalry in minor ways, like holding and opening doors. To experience this fine man this way gives me hope and an inclination to want to know more about my neighbor of the past year.

The breeze from the wind hits my open pores and brings me out of my thoughts. I step back to close the door. The act of service is still on my mind, and I want to thank him for taking the time to do something so generous for me.

"*The way to a man's heart is through his belly.*"

My grandmother's sweet, soft voice sings through my thoughts, and I feel like I can hear her melodic laugh ever present; it causes a huge smile to cross my face. I wonder why that thought came to mind, but one thing's for sure: my Papa loved my grandmother wholeheartedly, and I wouldn't be surprised if it had been for her soul-clenching southern cooking. That was my favorite thing about weekends with my grandparents as a child, being here on Sundays to get a full, cooked-from-scratch dinner of Southern delicacies. There was always fried chicken, hand-battered and floured, sweet corn pudding, savory macaroni and cheese, and greens with the right amount of vinegar and a pinch of sugar—my mouth waters at the thought. I could even taste it and imagine Papa strolling in from the back door, hooting and hollering in delight and scooping my grandmother up in his arms while she completed his plate.

I could make an extra portion of dinner. Not that I'm trying to get in this man's heart or anything. I quickly ensure my fluttering heart that says otherwise.

"I'm cooking anyway, and it's my way of giving a small token of gratitude." I huff at myself, heading into my room. "Yes, it's that, it's all about gratitude." I keep telling myself this, but I find myself going back and forth to my closet between prepping dinner and debating which dress to wear. A *Dress*. Not leggings or jeans, but a dress. *It's Sunday, and you're inviting–well, planning to invite– someone over for dinner. I should put on a little bit of better clothes, right?*

It's a little after three when I have dinner simmering. It ends up being a feast: juicy roasted chicken breasts, savory long-grain rice seasoned with my favorite blends of herbs and spices, and my grandmother's collard greens. I warmed up some store-bought rolls to go on the side. I don't usually eat this heavy with the extra carbs or even cook this large of a portion for just myself, but after catching glimpses of Ace mowing and then doing his typical workout set, I figure he may be a man who burns through his calories in a sitting. Anything not eaten today I could eat during the week.

I decided on a green floral dress, too. I do a once-over of myself in the floor-length mirror that leans in the corner of my room, smoothing my hands down the form-fitting dress. It wasn't like skin to my body but hugs my petite body comfortably with a modest plunge in the front. Not having much time to think of my hair, it dried in its conditioner-heavy state, a curly, fluffy, and frizzy combination, and I love her. Without giving myself too much time to think of another way to spruce up my look, I move through the house and out the back to extend my dinner invitation to Ace.

"This is only a dinner," I remind myself, taking inventory that my thoughts are still running over how I look as I cross my yard to his, both manicured to perfection.

There's a moment of silence after I knock on his door before my pupils adjust to the velvet skin of his bare chest as he nears the door. If I were to say this wasn't the perfect sight, the breath that gets stuck in my throat and the way my eyelids droop slightly with admiration would contradict that idea. I breathe out and scan my eyes over his velvet chocolate face as he opens the door. *God, I could indulge in this chocolate every day.* I flutter my eyelids to mentally shoo away my invading thoughts and curve my lips into a smile, hoping to disguise my passing thoughts.

"Hey," Ace greets, matching my smile with a bright one of his own. His eyes show the confusion of my presence.

"Hey. I just wanted to come by and invite you to…uh..you to dinner." I stammer over my words, distracted by the full view of Ace, standing in nothing but a towel that barely wraps around his muscle-bulging hips. He must catch my gaze because he grips the side of it as if it were slipping. *Focus, Sade, focus.* "After you get dressed–*ugh*–I mean…"

Ace chuckles at me, clamoring over my words, and saves the moment. "I would be dumb to turn down a home-cooked meal. It beats the takeout I was getting ready to order."

I laugh off my embarrassment, yet still silently cursing myself out. Here I am, acting like a young girl seeing her first Calvin Klein underwear ad. *I am a grown-ass woman and have seen a half-naked man before.* Granted, it's been a long–very long–time since I have, but I have, but not like *him*. Most men I date are athletic or at least have a sense of wellness, not that I have anything against other men. Ace, however, is a different kind of wellness man. I've watched him lift his barbell, holding what looks like a ton of weight with one hand, starting from on the ground and then standing fully erect and then back down, only to repeat with the other side of his body. He's the definition of a supreme god-Olympian kind of man.

"Cool." I reel myself back in. "So, see you in a few..?"

"Twenty minutes tops. Is that alright, Miss Sade?" He leans on the open door and gleams a Billy Dee Williams smile at me like I'm Diana in the *Mahogany* movie.

"Yeah." My voice comes out soft and dreamy, falling into the trance of his smile, but in a split second, I am back with a bone to pick with him. "But leave that 'Miss' talk here. I am far too young and fine for that kind of formality."

I walk off without waiting for him to respond with a small saunter to my walk. I can hear him laughing as I walk off, but I can also feel his presence watching me. At that moment, I felt like I was in the *Waiting to Exhale* scene where Gloria is walking off from her new neighbor Marvin, wondering if he was watching her walk away.

I hope he's not watching me walk away. The famous line from the movie cuts through my thoughts, and I chuckle at myself because I am literally wondering the same thing, fighting the urge to look back to confirm my suspicion. I falter to my curiosity and glance over my shoulder. He is watching and still wearing that Billy Dee smile. He catches my eye contact and shoots a quick wink. I blush, and a heat that's nowhere to be found in the current weather spirals up my body.

"He's watching," I murmur as I turn my sight back to my path and bite my lip to fight the growing smile back.

* * *

The descent of the sky is going from fuschia to a deep purple as the sun sets. Ace and I find ourselves still at my kitchen table with remnants of the smell of cooked food and the lavender vanilla candle I have burning intertwined together. It wafts through the air through the ceiling fan above the kitchen table. Besides the sound of Ace scraping the plate in front of him clean, my typical Sunday playlists of Neo Soul and R&B singers croon from the speakers in the living room. These familial tunes create the melody of a well-lived home, a sound that hadn't filled this home since my grandparents occupied it. I smile at the fond memory and the view of Ace leaning back into his chair, looking full like a stuffed teddy bear.

"Has anybody ever told you that you cook like an old Southern grandma?"

"There you go, calling me an old lady again." I dart a side eye at him and screw my mouth to the side.

Ace shrugs his broad shoulders to his ears. "Hit dogs holler."

I'm gagged by his rebuttal and burst into a howling laugh. "Now *that's* an old saying, old man!"

"We're even then!" Ace roars into a laugh, setting off another round of laughter from me. We've been having this kind of banter ever since dinner started. As soon as he sat at the table, it was like two familiar souls finding each other, jumping into the conversation, and never missing a beat. We talked about everything, current affairs, about each other, but most importantly, we laughed. I love to laugh, and it was a bonus to know he has a sense of humor and wit that matches mine.

"All jokes aside. This," Ace's laugh has trailed off, and he's surveying his empty plate with his finger. "This was great. I appreciate you."

I purse my lips into a subtle smile, his words of appreciation prickling my skin. "I'm glad you enjoyed it. It was the least I could do to show my gratitude."

"Slight work." His dark irises are fixated on me. He doesn't know it, but they are cutting through the layers of my skin and piercing my heart. I don't know what it is about his gaze, but they send my heart swinging like a pendulum, him being the point of attraction. I cut my eyes down to my empty plate and smooth the napkin in my lap, working to regain my senses while debating if I should say what my heart wants to say next.

"You're welcome to dinner anytime." My heart wins over my mind just as the words float out of my mouth. It pauses a beat like it is rethinking taking charge while waiting for his response.

"I'll do you one better." I look at him with curious eyes. "I fry a mean whiting. I'll help with the next one….next Sunday?"

The last part of his sentence comes out slow, and Skipper, also known as my beat-skipping heart, flips inside, wanting to blurt out my agreement for the following Sunday in excitement. My mind tags itself in, coaxing me to keep my cool. I nod my head and keep my subtle smile fixed.

"Sounds like a date." *A date?!* My mind explodes at the insinuation that this would be our first date....potentially? "Sunday sounds good."

    I was hoping that Ace didn't think I was trying to push the idea of a date on him, but by the way, Ace's smile grows; maybe the idea of it being…a date…isn't bad. Maybe the sparks setting off when we are around each other aren't just seen by me. Maybe my heart isn't the only one somersaulting. Maybe our eyes are communicating the same interest in each other. Just maybe.

III

Third Sunday

Sade

He asks me to ride with him to Lovey's Bay, and I'm in here fretting over my clothes. And I am doing just that, standing in front of my mirror, doing a quick once over of the white and navy pinstripe linen dress I chose to wear on the trip to Lovey's Bay. I fiddle with the ruffled, off-the-shoulder top, ensuring it sits comfortably below my moisturized shoulder. The rays of the beaming sun reflect over my rose quartz, and my heart's center begins to throb at the thought of Ace, a feeling that has been growing in strength over the last week.

After dinner last Sunday, we exchanged numbers. One 'good morning' text turned into two and then to every morning this week, and they all followed with long text threads filled with questions about what each other likes and dislikes and everything in between. I learned he took over his father's auto shops after moving to Florida and loves him very much. He didn't tell me this, but I can tell by how he talks about him and his weekly conversations with him. It's admirable how he stepped in for his father, although he really didn't have to after knowing how their relationship once was. His ability to understand that his father only did what he knew and was able to forgive him is an attractive trait.

I chuckle at the thought of us carrying on like teenage sweethearts, up all night on the phone, "Whatcha doing?" and "Are you sleeping?" every few minutes, neither one of us wanting to hang up first. It's been a long time since I carried on like this with a man. Hell, this type of feeling, butterflies in my stomach, the anticipation for the next interaction since being in high school. It's a refreshing sensation that makes me feel alive in more places than just my heart. Perhaps the rumble of his baritone plays a part in that as well.

I hear the bright ding of my text notification and come out of my thoughts. I know who it may be texting, and a satisfying smile reaches my cheeks when it's confirmed.

Ace: I gassed up the Pacer.

I burst into an echoing laughter at his reference to a classic Martin episode. This is the kind of thing we are doing now, reciting TV or movie lines to express ourselves. With just that quote, I quickly decoded that he was outside waiting for me.

Sade: I get to ride in the Pacer? On the way, Coley Cole!

I click the buttons on the side of my phone to put it to sleep, letting another chuckle slip through and grab my small crossbody. I usually see him in a blacked-out Dodge Charger in passing, but today, he is not in a Pacer but a big black Cadillac Escalade. I wonder how I would get into this big body SUV until Ace comes into view, walking toward the passenger side. As I reach him, the scent of tobacco and vanilla envelopes me through the passing wind, lifting my gaze to the culprit. His charming smile gleams bigger than I've seen before, showcasing a dimple at the left corner of his mouth. It gives his face a boyish touch to his very masculine physique that never ceases to show itself in anything that adorns his body. Like today, he wears a canyon copper button-up shirt with his hulking biceps curved from the bottom of the sleeves and a pair of khaki slim-fit shorts that hug his well-built glutes. *It's something about a man who understands that every day isn't an arm day.* I blush away my keen observations as he opens the passenger side door for me and offers his hand to help me into the truck.

Lovey's Bay is about a forty-five minute drive from Stonecrest but well worth the drive for its Sunday farmer's market. Local growers and vendors gather in the town's center, bringing their locally grown fruits and vegetables, honey, wine, you name it. With Lovey's Bay not too far from the Atlantic Ocean, the market is well known to have some of the freshest seafood. Ace thought it would be a good road trip to gather ingredients for our dinner tonight, and I obliged with not much hesitation. I liked the idea of having a little more time with him today than just for dinner.

"So…tell me something I don't know about you." When I ask Ace this question, we are about ten miles from Lovey's Bay. We had been talking the whole way down with Ace's 90s hip-hop playlist as our soundtrack. Although his taste in Biggie, A Tribe Called Quest, and Wu-Tang is a vibe, I can't lie; he's an even better vibe that I want to keep listening to.

He huffs out a stifling chuckle and gives me a quick side-eye. He is wearing a mischievous grin plastered on his face, and I'm wondering what he will say. "Hmm. I think it's the perfect time to tell you…my name is not Ace."

My heart drops to the pit of my stomach as if I was on a roller coaster on its way down its version of the pit of hell, caught off guard by his wild confession. Before I can verbally bug out, Ace's laughter cracks the silence between us, and he quickly continues.

"Wait. Don't trip. Ace is an acronym for my full name, Aeran Christian Eddings."

My mind races, computing the name algorithm he just presented me with while my gut settles with the knowing that Ace was telling me the truth and not some psycho I needed to flee the car away from. Truthfully, I have a similar truth I am holding from him as well that causes me to giggle at the coincidence.

"Since we are confessing things," I begin my confession with a purposeful slowness. I glance at him to see his laughing face turn emotionless as he double-takes in my direction. "I'm not necessarily Sade."

"What?" Ace laughs nervously and holds his puzzled gaze on me a little longer as he rounds the corner to the street that leads to the farmer's market.

I bite my lip to hold back the giggle I want to let out and lean against the window to get a complete look at him. "Sade's my middle name. I was born Amelia Sade Gresham."

Ace's mouth grows wide as he mouths, 'Wow,' followed by laughter straight from his chest, and it causes me to break into a giggling fit. "I guess we can see we are officially on government name status."

"Right," I agree, still snickering at this whole debacle. I can't make up this scenario if I want to, but this oddly diminishes the last guard of unfamiliarity between us. The truck comes to an easy stop as we glide into the park on the side of the green open field that hosts the farmer's market.

I can get used to this. My mind sings as Aeran helps me out of the vehicle, continuing to emulate a true gentleman. From the cringing salutation of 'Miss' that I've finally gotten him to stop saying to me to the holding of doors, they are small gestures but something I appreciate experiencing over the last few weeks. I look up at Aeran after I ground myself on the soil, his rich brown irises glinting from the high noon sun. They warm me a few degrees more than the sun's effect and confirm the sentiment that I could get used to having a man around who valued and respected the woman in me.

The market is bustling today; it's expected because it is a beautiful day with no chances of precipitation. Days like this bring the people in droves, but at this moment, although busy, the crowd is not as thick as I suspect it will be in a couple of hours from now. An excitement grows from my soles to the beam of my smile as we get closer to the market set up, and I notice many of the vendors are black-owned businesses. I love having an opportunity to support locals, especially as a small business owner myself. Being an entrepreneur, whether full or part-time, isn't for the faint of heart, and any time I can applaud a small business monetarily, I do. I immediately gravitate to a red-clothed table with crystals, incense, and jewelry. The sista behind the table, who wears a multicolor print scarf wrapped high upon her head, a black casual dress, and jewelry up her sleeveless arms, greets me with a beautiful bright smile, displaying a middle gap that adds to her uniqueness.

"Hey, sista, I'm Desni. Let me know if you see anything," she greets me. She didn't have to convince me to intake her table; the sparkle of the rigid raw crystals pulled me in.

"Absolutely," I say, my voice trailing as my eyes meet a long string of beads of tiny, vivid blue and white polished crystals. I run my fingers over them and subtly feel my energy shift.

"Looks like your energy is calling for my favorite piece, Love's Ocean."

I look at her with inquiry and bashfully smile at the name of the piece I am drawn to. "Sounds interesting. Tell me more."

Her smile takes on a bit more sass. "The waist bead is made of blue tiger's eye and white jade crystals. Blue Tiger's Eye is a great calming stone. It promotes clarity and communication and supports a healthy libido, while the white jade enhances the feeling of love within your life. Great sex, great love life, the perfect ebb and flow to a personal ocean, ya know? The Universe must be saying something to ya."

I release a soft chuckle as I move the crystals of the waist beads in between my thumb and forefinger, taking in descriptions of them. Sex and love have been distant relatives in my life over the past few years. In fact, the last man that I had relations with was Donovan, a guy I dated until my grandmother passed. It was casual yet somewhat exclusive. I'm not a woman who dates multiple men at a time, especially if I'm intimate with them, but how I felt about him wasn't enough to want me to commit exclusively to him in a solid relationship. He was a great guy, but something was missing in our connection. It was my grandmother's passing and finding out about the inheritance and the trust fund my grandfather left for me that sparked the finality of us. Remembering the love that my grandparents had for each other that exuded in the decisions they made for the well-being of their family lineage highlighted that I didn't feel that kind of desire with Donovan. I didn't see us growing old together and creating a legacy for generations. That's what I wanted, and wasting my time and Donovan's wouldn't get me any closer to it.

"How much is it?" I hear the words come out of my mouth before I register them with my mind. I don't even think my mind is in the decision-making of this impulse buy, just my growing heart and the flutter in my womb. I don't remember the amount she told me, but I paid her with my virtual wallet app on my phone. She thanked me and began to wrap the waist beads in blue paper.

"Found something?" Aeran's voice comes in close behind me. I turn to find him towering over me, only a few inches away. He's peering down at the table of crystals.

"Yeah, some waist beads."

"Tell me about them."

I turn to face him, my face bubbling with a constricted smile. I was unsure if I should tell him all I knew about the crystals on the waist beads, but my daring side took over. "The crystals, tiger's eye, and jade represent love and your libido."

His eyes slightly narrow and grow with a sense of desire that meets the same lust in my pupils. I feel my breath shorten as his full, deep pink lips curve into a sly grin. He reaches up, trails his fingers over a curl that had fallen into my gaze, and then gently moves it as he glides his large, slightly rough hand to palm the side of my face. His thumb glides soothingly over my skin, sending my body flush. "Hmm. Is that right, beautiful?"

"Mmhmm," is all that I manage to say as the feeling in my body begins to diminish and our surroundings start to blur out of focus, leaving just us linked by the pulsing fondness that keeps bouncing between us. My pupils move between his eyes and his lips, both seeming to grow closer to me, and when I feel the heat and scent of his breath, I know this is not a daydream but happening for real. I am poise and wanting for the collide of our lips.

"Ahem." a soft clearing of someone's voice cuts into the moment, causing me to blink back into the present moment in the bustling farmer's market. "Sista, your bag is ready."

I swivel on my toes back to sis with the headscarf, slightly embarrassed. She meets me with a knowing eye and an approving smile. She extends her arm out to me with the bag in hand. I retrieve it, thanking her again.

"Enjoy your beads," she sings, looking between me and Aeran. I blush and turn away, leading us toward the fresh meats and produce.

Ace

*W*as that too much? She didn't seem to be offended...did she? Man, I hope I didn't fuck that up. My mind is bogged down with thoughts of our near collision of lips just moments ago. I trail behind Sade, watching her hips sway as my carnal side still runs wild. I grumble at myself for being unable to reign my beast in, but it's been hard, literally and figuratively, since we've increased communication over the past week.

Sade is beautiful physically, especially today, with her cloud of curls framing her dewy, supple face, her glassy lips making way for her bright smile. The way her dress drapes her petite frame, subtly highlighting the satin skin of her shoulders, cinching at her trim waistline, respectfully exposing the roundness of her bubble butt when she walks. However, the depth of her mind, the way she catches my jokes without even knowing they're jokes, and the ease of simply talking to her make the beast in me crave her. Some would call me a sapiosexual, but I would say I like a woman who knows how to use her mind. That moment was pure attraction, and I'm sure it wasn't just on my end. When she turned to face me, I could see it in her eyes; I could feel it vibrating between us like some hidden magnetic field, and I just went for it. I would bet anything we would've connected in just an electric kiss if homegirl hadn't spoken up.

We finish the rest of our shopping for dinner within the hour and try to keep things nice and friendly. I grabbed several pieces of freshwater whiting, probably too many for tonight, but I could either cook a few for later this week or freeze. While Sade peruses a vendor with organic vegetables, my phone vibrates with an incoming call from Pops. For a moment, I thought to let the call go to voicemail, but when I saw that Sade was content in choosing vegetables and conversing with the older woman who managed the table, I stepped to the side and answered the call.

"Hey, Pops, what's going on?"

"Soaking up some rays and watching the ladies play!"

I breathe out a hearty laugh at my dad's never-ending wordplay. "Pops, you're a mess, but I believe you're doing just that."

"And you know it. Whatcha got goin' on? You sound like you're out for once."

I take notice of the subtle chatter around me and the live band in the background before taking another glance towards Sade when he says this. Sade peeps my gaze and flashes me a smile before returning to her conversation. I debate whether I want to mention to Pops that I was out with her, but knowing him, he probably already assumes I am.

"Yeah, I went out to Lovey's Bay today."

"Lovey's Bay? That Sade girl got you open, huh? Out at *Lover's Bay*." He cackles at his knowing. He was correct about Lovey's Bay being known as Lover's Bay for its intimate vibe fitting for a nice, intimate day date, and maybe with the point of me being a little smitten over Sade.

"Ahh, something like that, Pops." I force out a stifled laugh at his accuracy and rub the top of my head. "But yeah, Sade and I came out for the farmer's market. Grab some things for a little kickback later."

"Mmhmm. I see you listened to me."

"Listen to you about what?"

"About catching that little birdie called Love before she flaps on away."

Here he goes. I roll my eyes to the sky as a smile curves over my face, remembering our conversation a few weeks back.

Love is fleeting...

"I mean, we're just chillin', Pop. Enjoying each other." The clouds in my head form the scenes of Sade's laughing face and then me in bed on the phone with her, letting her breathy, sleepy voice guide my mind in wonders of what she looks like when she's in bed fighting sleep or what she chooses to sleep in. I snap back into reality as Sade approaches me with a couple of clear bags I can make out as a bushel of asparagus and a few sweet potatoes. "Hey, I gotta go, Pops. I'll hit you later?"

"Aight, boy. I love you, and make sure you seal that deal with a smokin' kiss, ya hear?" Pops cackles at himself again, and I chuckle before saying our goodbyes.

"That seemed like a fun convo." She lets out a nervous laugh. Maybe she was wondering who was on the phone, and even if she wasn't, I had no plans of hiding anything from her.

"Every conversation with Pops is a wild one. That's my guy." I snicker, thinking about Pops, and she joins in, her nervous energy dissipating. I look down at her with a smirk, noticing that she is wondering about my call, and it secures a knowing that we are in alignment with the growing fondness. A more profound comfort in this knowing settles in my chest, and I lightly pinch her hand with my thumb. She looks up at me briefly, her face warming, and then intertwines her tiny fingers between my long fingers. The feel of her baby-soft palm against mine doubles the heat that permeates.

Just as we returned to the beginning of the vendor circle, a wine seller caught my eye. He is a young brother who looks close in age. He has a vibe that gives off that he's from up North; the fade and the class Nas hook part solidifies that. He wears a brown and black tribal button-up with a large copper Ankh around his neck. His dope vibe was enough for me to glance over his wine collection.

"What's up, man? Joaquim," he introduces himself as I come up to his table, extending his hand for an obvious dap up.

I dap him up and return the greeting. "Sup. Ace. I see you slinging wine, eh?"

"Fasho, brotha. I ferment my wine with a base of varying fruits."

I feel Sade's presence is on my side as Joaquim offers a tasting of the two of the three wines he has on display. I turn to Sade with a tilt toward the sampling to ask if she'd like to sample. She nods with a warm smile, and Joaquim passes her a sample of a pale gold wine. I take the other sample from him that has a slight red hue.

"Sis, you have the "Candied Peach" which is a white peach wine with hints of honey, and you, bro, you have the "Apple Iris," an apple wine."

She watches me as I watch her, and we both indulge in the sample, our eyes never disconnecting. I watch her suck in her rotund bottom lip to taste all of the essence of the wine. As her bottom lip plops free, my mind's eye creates a new scene in which I pull her supple lip into my mouth to suck away the peach flavor. My eyes narrow at the hunger in my thoughts of her. I see her chest rise as she slowly fills it with air, and I wonder what thoughts she enjoys.

"Yeah…" Joaquim elongates the word. I redirect my attention to him, where I find him darting his eyes between Sade and me with his silent questions. He lets out a couple of chuckles that tell me he is wondering what naughty mind fuck he just witnessed. "So what y'all think?" Sade and I both snicker at the moment, clearing away the searing fire between us.

"Yeah, this one is cool," I answer first, placing the empty sample cup on the table. I meet Sade's eyes for her response.

"Yeah, I like this one too, a lot." Her voice sings soft, sultry, and airy. It's music to my ears. She's my siren, and I am her submissive captive.

"We'll take two for the lady," I request, letting my eyes linger for a few more seconds on Sade before I return my attention to complete the sale. I don't think we will finish two bottles tonight, but Sade is a whirlwind of magic. Without saying too many words, she can get anything out of me.

* * *

"And, ooooh, you're gonna love me…!" Reaching for a shaky falsetto, Sade sings Teyana Taylor's song, swinging her hips in a two-step to the beat, her half-empty glass of wine steady in her right hand.

I throw my head back in laughter, the back of my heavy head connecting to the back of the couch. I barely feel the thud of my head on the sofa; the three glasses of wine have me feeling light as a feather and heavy simultaneously. I close my eyes and let out what I hope will be a sobering breath, but as I open my eyes again, I find it isn't. My blurry vision clears to a giddy Sade whose face is lit with a big smile that transfers to my face. I didn't see her put her glass down, but she did at some point. She grabs my shirt collar with both hands, pulling me from the couch with a force I didn't know she had.

"Come dance." She stumbles back from the force of pulling me up, but I catch her fall before it happens, scooping my arm around her back and pulling her close. Her breast connects to my chest, and I feel her slightly hardened nipples press against me. She throws her arms around my neck, not even noticing her near fall, and continues to mouth the lyrics to the song. I two-step to her somewhat off movements, my smile unfaltering. I'm not much of a dancer, but for her, I will try not to stumble over my two left feet, an even more challenging feat with being wine-wasted.

Could I have imagined the night going like this at the start of the day? Parts of it. Us having a good day at the farmer's market and then collaborating on dinner? Yes. But the increasing coziness of our spirits with one another to the point we are in the middle of her living room, two wine bottles down, drunkenly dancing? Nah. But I can't say I'm unhappy with how the night is panning out. *I can get used to this.* I nod to the thought and run my hands down the small of her back, setting them just above the tempting curve of her ass. She slowly blinks up at me as a flirty smirk takes over her face, not breaking her steps but slowing them down as the song fades into October London's "Back to Your Place."

"Woo," I let out as the beat drops. "This dude right here is the truth. Bringing back that Marvin Gaye smoothness."

"Marvin! Please believe me!" Sade yells out in her rendition of Juanita from *Baby Boy*. I cackle at her silliness and even know what she was referencing. This kind of thing makes me fall even more for her.

"You're so silly, baby." The name of endearment floats from my mouth seconds after my mind registers and decides it doesn't care. Sade looks up at me, her cheeks puffed in the cute way she does when she is fighting away her blush, tightening her lips in containment. I couldn't resist. I close the space between our faces and plant a sweet peck on her lips. Her chocolate brown irises are sober as they widen softly in the realization that I kissed her and then softened as she pecks me once and then twice before our lips crash into each other with a zeal that has been brewing all day. The beast in me growls at the intensity, and I move my hands to cup the sides of her face to deepen the kiss. She parts her lips, and I take her in, swiping my tongue across hers with my carnal instincts taking over.

It felt like a movie scene as the song changed to Usher, "Can You Handle It?" as my inner beast took over, wanting to feast on this pretty brown thing before me. I disconnect from the kiss. Sade searches my eyes for answers as to why I stopped, and I narrow my eyes with prowess intentions taking over. I take my tongue and swipe long across her plump bottom lip before taking it into my mouth and sucking off the faint remnants of the peach wine. As I release her lip, she releases a soft moan, lifting her gaze at me with a spark I hadn't been introduced to until now.

"I've been wanting to see what that peach tastes like." The words rumble from a low voice, carrying many contexts.

I could hear the crackling and then the pop of the heat between us that signified that it was too hot and too late to turn back the heat, and I think she could, too. Our lips crash into each other one moment, and the next, we collide on the couch with Sade straddling my wide hips. In another moment, I'm kissing, sucking, and nipping at her neck while her hands massage my scalp through my curls, releasing pleasured moans. I find my hands roaming over her smoothness of ass underneath the skirt of her dress. She rocks into me, her center making contact with my hard manhood. I let out a hungry moan, wanting to let my inner beast take over completely, but only if she wanted it, too.

She does. She lifts slightly and begins to unbutton my shorts, keeping her gaze on mine, ensuring me that she does want this. I raise to assist her in pulling down my shorts and briefs, releasing my lengthy, swollen sword. I see her look down at him and bite her lip with satisfaction. She proceeds to unbutton my shirt and runs her hands down the dips and crevices of the muscles that inhabit my chest before climbing off of me to remove her dress, revealing her bare breasts and nearly naked body. The only thing that dresses her petite, ballet dancer body is a thin lace bikini-style panties. I puff out an exhale and shake my head at the astonishing beauty in front of me before pulling her back into my lap, landing her perky breast in the vicinity of my mouth. Just where I want them. I palm her back with my right hand, cup her left breast in my hand, and take it into my mouth. I suck and lick her nipple into a hardened submission and then give her right breast the same love, all while she moans a song that takes over the now-silent room.

I want her. Oh, I do. But I want her to know I value her at this moment. I reach for my pants and pull out my wallet and then a condom. A smile of appreciation creeps onto her face as she places her hand over mine and retrieves the condom. She unwraps and rolls it down my stiff shaft slowly, then straddles me again, moves her thong to the side, and slides down on me. I suck in the cool air at the same speed as she descends, slow, feeling the suction of her walls grip my dick and relax when she's full of me. We let out an exhilarated moan in unison, both at the feeling of the warmth, the depth, the slickness. She rocks back and forth on my dick, and I lay my head back in a foggy pleasure, massaging the sides of her bubble butt with each roll of her hips. With each roll, I feel her budded flower rub into me, and each time it does, her moan becomes more audible, her hips rocking faster and with more force. I grip the sides of her thong as if I want to reign her in, but that's the last thing I want. I want to gain a little control so I can pump my long length in her ocean as I meet her roll. Each time she lifts, I thrust a louder moan out of her.

"Oh..shit.." Thrust.

"Ahh.." Thrust.

"Oh my—*thrust*— god—*thrust*—, Ace..." Thrust. Thrust. Thrust.

With the last thrust, her dainty panties pop from the force of my grip, and the bounce of her ass and all control in motion is gone. Our pants. Our moans. The slaps of our thighs. The squish of her wetness. It's a song that's on repeat and changes into a fast, uncontrollable tempo that comes to a climactic ending.

* * *

Zzzz...Zzzz...Zzzz

I'm awake to a muffled sound ringing in my ear like an alarm clock. As I become more alert, I realize it's a faint cellphone vibration. I furrow my eyebrows, scanning my surroundings for clues to where I am. Tilting my head to the side, a fluffy curl tickles my bearded chin, and I glance down to see a half-naked Sade, scantily covered by a furry blanket, and it all comes rushing back to me. The farmer's market. Dinner. Two bottles of wine…and her immaculate body on top of mine. The echo of her moans in my mind tries to force my slight morning wood to jump, but I gather the mental control and clarity I need to get up from the compromising position. Not that I want to; the feeling of Sade resting on my chest feels nothing short of heaven, but the slight guilt of letting things go to the extremes they did last night kicks in.

Sade stirs and blinks her eyes open, and it's enough for me to feel comfortable to rub her back lightly and lift, knowing that she is somewhat awake. The look on her face goes from confusion to realization with a little bit of "Oh..fuck" in the mix of it all. It was very similar to my line of thought when I came through. She wraps the blanket a little more snugly around her, covering her breasts, and hurries to the opposite corner of the couch.

"Good morning," she says, a faint smile settling on her face, her eyes darting from the articles of clothing scattered on the floor, empty wine glasses on the center table, and then to me.

"Good morning." My smile and eyes find hers, and I let them settle for a moment, wanting to ensure her that my genuine fondness for her is still here before I say anything else that could be interpreted otherwise. I part my lips to speak slowly to be intentional about my wording. "I think I overstayed my welcome and should go."

Her smile stays firm, but her brows furrow slightly before settling back into their rested state. "You didn't, but I do understand. It's Monday. Back to the real world."

Monday. It is Monday, and it dawns on me that I've only seen her consistently on a Sunday over the last few weeks. Still, sitting here, looking at her natural morning glow and frizzy mane billowing over her like a crown, I can picture waking up to this sight every day. I can see myself greeting her happily every morning with a kiss, even with morning breath. I can see myself wanting to hear her sultry moan as I make love to her every morning. Even on a Monday morning, Sade's presence is still sweet, like a Sunday.

Without much more conversation, we both start moving around. She disappears into the depths of her home, and I can hear the bathroom faucet running and the start of an electric toothbrush. I dress while thinking of what to say or if I should leave without saying anything. The latter isn't an option; the last I want to do is leave her with questions, but I'm stuck on how to be with her as we unintentionally moved into a different space between us last night. *What is this space we are in now?*

Moments later, Sade appears in her satin robe with a quaint smile. She grabs the two empty wine glasses, and I follow her to the kitchen, stopping at the back door, still debating how to leave. I turn around, and she's standing mere feet away from me.

"Seal that deal with a smokin' kiss.."

Pops' voice resounds clearly in my mind as I close the space between us, cup her face with my hands, and plant a smooch of definiteness to her lips: firm, with intention, and sealing in that she is more than just one Sunday night to me. I linger on her lips briefly before planting one more for extra security. Sade bats her eyes open, and she gleams with contentment at me. She sinks into my heart just a bit more from that sight.

"I'll see you later...*Amelia.*" I cut the steaming air by joking about calling her by her first name. It catches her off guard, causing her to giggle at the aftermath of the realization. I peck her again before turning around and walking out of the door.

Once I step into my yard and hear her door close, I stop in the middle and breathe out a breath full of peace…of completeness. It's a wholeness that settles in the seat of my soul that I had never felt before. For some reason, I can picture my Pops laughing and nodding at me with a sense of "I told you so" written on his face, and I chuckle. *Maybe, Pops, maybe.* I remove my phone from my pocket to call him but notice I have a voicemail from an unknown Florida number. Puzzled, I click the message to listen to the message on the speaker:

"This message is for Mr. Aeran Eddings. I am Claudia Jones at the Sunnyveiw Senior Community, and you are listed as Mr. Quincy Eddings' point of contact. I'm so sorry to have to call and leave you a message like this. We found him unresponsive this morning and without a pulse—"

IV

Fourth Sunday

Sade

I don't know if I can do anything or even if I should.

This last week has been…different. After the night with Ace, I could have never seen that we would be back to where we were just a month ago, hardly saying a few words to each other. But could I blame him?

I revisit the memorable Sunday with Ace every time I begin to fret over the distance between Ace and me, looking for clues in his personality and interaction with me that would show signs that he shuts down, but there were none. That Sunday, we were both all the way open, hearts on our sleeves, eyes speaking our sweet and sensual things we dared not to say in public, and when our lips finally touched, it solidified that, oddly, I was his, and he was mine. I feel crazy just thinking about that kind of possession, but it's true; I know what I felt, not just physically but emotionally and mentally, in all the things we shared that day, including our intimate moments. We were drunk, for sure, but I wasn't drunk enough that I wasn't aware of what I was doing, who I was doing it with, and that I wanted every moment..and he did too, right?

He's grieving.

My mind keeps trying to lull me away from the mental chaos of overthinking a fact that is true: he is grieving, but I didn't know this until Wednesday, after not hearing from him since Sunday. There were no good morning texts or a reply to my good morning text, which I thought I'd send after 24 hours without one. It wasn't until Wednesday that I mustered up the courage to call him after feeling ghosted. I figured that if I didn't hear anything, I would chuck up the feelings to be nothing but lust and try to carry on without giving him a side eye the next time I saw him in his backyard. When I heard the line pick up, my heart skipped at the opposite of the rejection I was expecting, but I almost regretted calling when I listened to the gruff in his voice and the curtness in his words. He was straight to the point with a one-word response to how he was doing until I asked him what was up with him.

"My father is dead."

I remember my breath catching and my heart sinking at his revelation. "I-I'm so sorr—"

"It's all good. But I can't do this. If I had answered his call Sunday night as opposed to…maybe I would've, maybe I could've.."

I recall him stumbling over his words, but I understood the implication that I was the reason he missed his father's last call, and that guilt cracked me inside, along with him in the same breath, breaking up what had not had a chance to begin yet.

My eyes tense at the swelling of tears lining my waterline as I replay our last conversation. I blink them away and return to the present moment, sitting at my kitchen table in front of a blue cookie tin of my grandmother's recipes. I look upon the now off-white sheets of lined paper that Grandma Amelia had handwritten her best recipes. One of the recipes pulls at me and my gaze, Papa's Heart Pound Cake.

I don't know if I can do anything or even if I should.
He's grieving.

The words keep running through my head, playing their game of tug of war, the award being the control of my mind and subsequent decisions. I blew out a heavy breath, figuratively blowing away the noise, and followed my heart's desire to try my hand at the recipe. Pulling the sheet of paper from the tin, I scan the list of the ingredients, making a mental note that I have everything it calls for, and then stop on a line of words that were not necessarily instructions.

Add a dollop of your whole heart to the making of this cake. Cook it with love and love will always be near.

I smile at the directive and close my eyes where the image of Grandma Amelia and Grandpa Winston shows. The scene of them I always remember takes place here, at this very home, grandma peddling around the home while grandpa worked on something in the backyard, all for the betterment of the family. They were the epitome of unwavering love and my proud example of what I desire to have in my life. Grandpa Winston showed his love by being a trustworthy provider. I get my green thumb mostly from him as he always was in the small garden, tending and harvesting seasonal fruits and vegetables. He also worked a factory job that provided for Grandma and my mom and then, years later, helped support my mother and me. Grandma never had to lift a finger to work to keep the house afloat. On most occasions, she never had to drive as Grandpa Winston was the chauffeur to wherever she wanted to go, no huffing with irritation at any stop or request. Grandma Amelia showed her love back by being the ultimate caregiver. She had the biggest heart on her sleeve proudly when it came to her family, cooking Sunday dinners in which she had the family over, watching me when my mother needed help, and healing me when I was too sick to go to school. But her love for Grandpa was especially seen. She never questioned his decisions about our family, and from my viewpoint, I didn't see a reason for her to because everything seemed good. As an adult, I realized that was an example of being submissive to the one you trust with everything. Grandpa showed and proved his intentions to lead our family with care and good intentions. She stood firmly by his side, even up until his last days when, as she told me, he said to her that he didn't want her to be sad that he was going Home because his heart would always be here. She never wavered, never ceased, just continued to hold a forever-steady love.

Am I crazy to think that maybe Ace is worth that steadfast...?

I sigh with some irritation at the pin-drop silence after my thought. Of course, I didn't expect a response from myself or anything, with the overworking of my brain of scenarios of what would be if I did or didn't pursue the pang in my heart's center that, without relent, gets stronger every time I think about Ace. I thought about calling my mother, but although I love her, her toxic mindset about men would not entertain this fairy tale of love that my spirit wants to engage. I didn't want that poison trickling into all of my already uncertainties.

Love.

It's not necessarily on the level of love, but I know it's a level of longing to see if it could be love one day, what it would be like to flow on the wave my heart is riding on. Even with the bit of fluttering in my stomach of guilt when I think about him missing his father's last call while being occupied with me, my soul speaks louder than it, saying that I did nothing to contribute to the fate of things.

I read over the last bit of the recipe again about cooking with love and love being always near. I registered my final answer to my heart's call: to bake the cake with all of my condolences, all of my empathy, all of my understanding, all of my patience, all of my faith, and all of my heart.

Ace

The birds chirping outside indicate a lovely day out, but my aching, dry eyes remind me of the clouds that consume my home. I've had no desire to do anything but lay on this couch, mindless flick through streaming apps, just…be. I thought I would be able to handle death, considering I experienced the loss of my mother, but this level of shutdown, I didn't expect. I can't tell if this kind of numbness is from consuming an exuberant amount of bourbon or because of my disbelief. This kind of silence pierces my psyche; it doesn't feel real, especially today when I haven't received my Sunday call from Pops.

It hurts most because I *just* got my Pops. Seventeen years ago, accurate, but not having him in my childhood, I felt like I just started experiencing my childhood with my Pops. The laughs were the personification of playing on the playground with my Pops; the advice was like getting the winning play from your football coach. It was all the building blocks to growing as a man, and I feel like he left right when amid my figurative adulthood. How do I navigate through what life has for me next now without Pops?

I squeeze my eyes tight, fighting back the speck of water that wants to fall, just as my body produces a frustrated growl at the situation. I've never felt this alone and confused. It feels like my chest has been carved open right down the middle, and my heart ripped out with no warning, but it was. After a good damn Sunday, God decided to shred it to dust with the news of my father—a bittersweet Sunday.

Although I want to wallow in my sorrows, my stomach pangs from neglect of nourishment. I reluctantly pull myself up to rummage through my bare refrigerator for anything to satisfy it. The house is shaded with translucent darkness as the sun sets, although no sun is in sight. The sky is covered with an overcast that confirms the impending storm I remember hearing during a news segment. There's this saying that the first rain after someone's death is when their spirit goes Home. I look over to the sealed package that contains my father's ashes with the devastating realization of this spiritual revelation coming to fruition today.

I couldn't get myself to open the box, so it sits on my kitchen table until I can, whenever that day will be. I avert my eyes away from my misery and open the refrigerator, grabbing the sliced turkey and cheese to prepare a sandwich. After I slap it together, I slump into the cold wooden chair at the kitchen table to eat in my melancholy. My phone chimes with a text alert. I don't rush to see what it is, but when I decide to look, I see a message from Sade.

Sade: I left you something at your back door. It's covered if you don't get this message before the rain. Hopefully, it will soothe your pain.

I remain expressionless, looking down at the blue bubbled message, in part feeling like an ass for shutting her out and somewhat blaming her for the missed call from my Pops on his last day. It wasn't her fault, nor mine, as my phone was on vibrate; I probably would've missed it no matter what, but it's the fact that I did. And because it was with her. I promised myself that when Pops and I grew close, I would not miss an opportunity to converse or spend time with him. We missed too many of those opportunities, so it broke me when I missed that one. It hurt me so much I hadn't even listened to the voicemail he left. I felt guilty for missing his call and for putting it on Sade. She didn't deserve it. She's been an angel in my life.

So, why are you shutting her out?

In my head, that voice sounds like my Pops, and it low-key weird me out, but it's a valid question I have been avoiding every time it comes to mind when I think of her. To be very honest with myself, I'm scared to lose anything else. I lost my Pops in a split second of a malfunction of his heart, and despite everything, I loved him just as hard as I loved my mom. I'm damn near losing my mind over this heartache; I don't know if I can fathom growing to love someone else to experience the same hurt.

Love.

I could see myself loving Sade heavily. The way my heart dips at the sight, the thought of her, I know it's on the way to succumbing to the dive. So it's just best that I stay in my yard, in my life, to avoid my pessimism and fear of messing things up. I can't lose this hard again.

Life and love are fleeting. That's the only thing I regret...not doing it with someone I love....

The words are too hauntingly clear now, and I'm bugging out at the sound of Pops's voice. I laugh out loud at myself for even entertaining that my mind's voice is my Pops, but then the thought of me having one last physical form of his voice on my phone that I have denied myself of listening to. I can't lie, I long to hear my Pops voice, so I swipe open my voicemail box, click the message, and place it on speaker to listen:

*"Aye, kid. Yeah, I know it's late, and I talked to ya earlier, but I was thinkin' about ya and gave you a call. Look at me, actually acting like a dad. *chuckles and then coughs* I'm proud of you, kid; I know I don't say it much, but I am. I wouldn't trust you with the business stuff if I had any thoughts that you would run it down to the ground when I'm finally gone. *chuckle* I owe you this anyway. But yeah, you make me proud, and I'm glad we can work things out.. spend some time. I love ya. *silence* Alright, let me stop rambling. I know you with my daughter-in-law-to-be, Sade, and don't debate me on it; I know she is. From the picture you sent me, she looks like ya mother, and if she's anything like her, you're falling for her like I fell for your mother. Keep that one close. I'll talk with ya."*

I blink, releasing the ocean of tears that pooled my eyes and didn't fight the breaking of the levy of my emotions. I sob like the little boy I feel like at this very moment. I hear the agony stumble from my throat as my Pops' admission of his love repeated over and over in my head.

"I love you too, Pops. I really do." I break the silence with my cracked, sorrowful voice. I support my head with my hands and my elbows astute on the table, supporting all the heaviness coming from me, ironically releasing the guilt slowly that I held at missing my dad's call, knowing that I have this voicemail that wraps every wondering thought I may have had about how my Pops felt about me. The thing about fathers is that they love hard, and they show it, but they do not nearly speak it just as deeply as they feel. It's needed. I needed it. I'm thankful I have this moment to play over again for the rest of my time without him.

I exhale soberly as the tears dry, and my body feels less heavy. There's thunder rumbling in the far distance, and I can hear the steady rain clattering against the roof. I remove myself from the chair, walk to the box, and rip the tape off, revealing my dad's black urn. I hold the cold, heavy metal in my hand and exhale again before placing him on the bookshelf in my second bedroom. It was safe to say my Pops has transitioned smoothly.

Keep that one close...

Sade's smiling face fades into my mind's eye, and a quickening hits my heart as my father's words echo through my head over and over like it's trying to pound some sense into me, and it does, the sense that I am on the verge of walking the path my father has been warning about through his calls all month. I was about to let the possibility of love slip through my fingers, and for what? There is no evident reason, just like Pops had no apparent reason, to let my mom and a full life, in his perception, slip away.

Lightning strikes something close enough that it rattles the home, and I remember Sade's text about something she left for me. I rush to the back door and swing it open, and after scanning the surroundings, an object diverts my attention to the ground. In front of me is a yellow cake on a stand covered with a topper. I retrieve it quickly and move toward the kitchen table to place it. I recover a note inside after taking the topper off just as the sweet aroma of the sugary icing hits my nose.

Aeran,

I didn't know what else to do but to bake you my grandmother's cake. She calls it Papa's Heart Pound Cake. I don't even know if I should have or if it will be received well, but here it is. She says to bake it with love, and love will always be near, so I followed the directions. In this cake, you'll find me, my heart, and what I think could grow into love. I'm really sorry about your loss, and I'm sorry a moment in time was missed. I hope this cake can bring you even an ounce of joy now.

Amelia

Before I can think, I'm rushing out the door, the heavy rain hitting my bare chest and drenching my basketball shorts, the only article of clothing I have on. When I realize this, I'm at the line between Sade and my yard, my feet squishing between wet, prickly grass and my limp, wet curls falling into my eyes.

What am I doing? I think, pushing my hair back and looking up at the dark sky, blinking away the raindrops as they hit my face. I look like a madman, I know it, but I'm stuck between a rock and a hard place of whether I should continue my way to her like this right now or waste another minute, another hour, another day without her.

"Ace?"

I snap forward and see Sade standing at her door underneath the awning that protects her from the rain. I lose my breath at her beauty. So simple and breathtaking. She stood with her hair free and flowing in a stretched-out afro that made her look like a version of Chaka Khan from her hair alone in a long kimono robe. She's looking at me with confusion, but I can see a glint of happiness in her eyes. It was enough for me to rush the last few feet of ground to her, but she met me before I could reach her, our bodies colliding with the force of our hurry. I grab her face and devour her lips to make her feel every longing I have built for her. I was missing my Pops, but I missed her joy, peace, and light just as much. She returns the kiss, deepening the passion as she parts her lips and allows her tongue to meet mine. We swipe with hunger at each other's tongues, with no never mind of the storm we stood in. I didn't want shelter from this rain; I just wanted her and would weather this storm for as long as she allowed me.

She pulls away, trying to catch her breath, and blinks at each droplet that makes its way to her face, letting out an amused laugh. "What are we doing in this rain?"

"I don't know, and I don't care now that I have you," I answer honestly, sharing in her amusement. I stare deep into her eyes, watching our future play in her pupils, and I want it. "I'm sorry, Sa—Amelia, I'm sorry." I stumble over my choice of what to call her, but Amelia feels right now because I want her to know I'm true to the words I am trying to form.

"It's okay," she interjects softly. "I know. I'm just happy you—"

"I always knew." It was my turn to interject. "The moment we sat down four weeks ago, I knew. You are the purest heart I've known. And I want to do this…to grow with you…see where this goes. I can't let life or the opportunity to love pass me by." I feel a tear escape thinking about my Pops' words again, and I hope that the steady rain disguises it from her.

Sade bites down on her lip, her pupils searching my eyes. I hold my eyes steady so she knows I'm for real. She has an expression that looks like happiness and a fight to hold back some hidden desire, and then it disappears as she throws her arms around my neck and pops up onto the ball of her feet to allow her wet lips to crash into mine. We lock lips with no sense of time, no care of the drenching of our clothes that is now clinging to our bodies, and for damn sure no care who may be viewing our show of affection for each other. I hoist Sade up swiftly, not breaking our connection until she is snug on my waist, and she is looking down at me with the same fire that blazes my eyes. She is so fucking beautiful, her curls now limp and falling past her shoulders and into her eyes. Our future keeps playing in her eyes, moment to beautiful moment. I even glimpse the babies I plan to plant in her womb one day. Without any other words, just the knowing that only we know, I walk us to her open backdoor to complete another sweet Sunday.

Ace

the end.

About the Author

Danielle Brooks (born Ashley Robinson) hails from Richmond, Virginia, with a long love for writing and reading since her school-age years. Her earliest memory of writing her first "book" was as a 5th grader in a simple five-subject notebook. She later found love in poetry, only sharing it with a few friends and family and occasionally in class. In 2023, Ashley decided to follow her pursuit to become an author, taking on her alter ego, Danielle Brooks, a name that pays homage to her identity and her family lineage. She currently still lives in Richmond with her two children, a host of family, and dear friends.